Fantastic Fairy Tales

SLEEPING BEAUTY

AF539049

An imprint of Om Books International

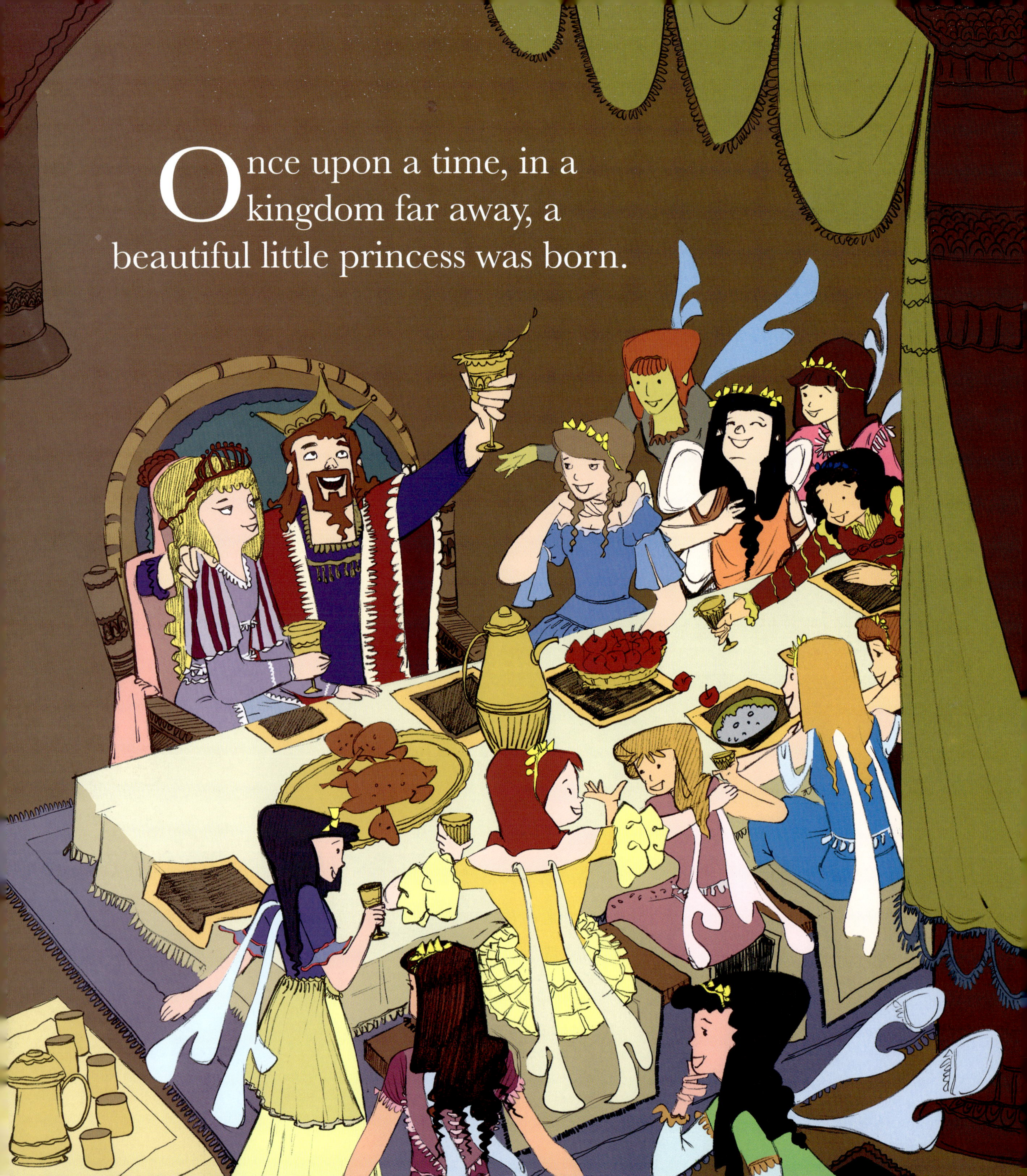

Once upon a time, in a kingdom far away, a beautiful little princess was born.

The king and queen held a grand feast and invited all the royal courtiers and the fairies of their kingdom.

Now, there were thirteen fairies in the kingdom, but when they sat down at the table, the king saw only twelve. He had forgotten to invite the thirteenth fairy! It wasn't really his fault, you see, the thirteenth fairy was not very friendly.

As the queen looked up anxiously, she saw the thirteenth fairy standing there and looking down angrily at them all.

"Please forgive us for not inviting you, dear fairy. Do join us now," pleaded the queen, but the thirteenth fairy just stood outside, sulking.

And then it was time for the fairies to bless the baby princess and shower her with gifts. The kind fairies blessed her with happiness, kindness, beauty and all manner of magical gifts.

Just as soon as the eleventh fairy had blessed the princess with love, the spiteful thirteenth fairy stepped up to her crib, an evil frown on her face.

“Did you all think I would so easily ignore this insult and forgive you for forgetting all about me?” she screamed.

“I will have my revenge!” she thundered, and the baby princess began to cry at the frightening voice.

“When the princess turns sixteen, she will prick her finger on a spindle and die!”

Everyone present there gasped in shock.

The twelve good fairies could not believe what their thirteenth sister had just done. She had cursed the princess, a tiny innocent baby! They had to do something to save the dear child from this dreadful fate.

The twelfth fairy came up and said, "My King and Queen, I have yet to give my blessings. This darling child will not die, but fall asleep for a hundred years, to be awakened only by the kiss of true love."

The king thanked the kind twelfth fairy, but he did not want any threat to his daughter's life. He ordered every spindle in and around the kingdom to be found and burnt to ashes.

Days, months and years passed by. The princess grew up to be a very beautiful young maiden. The blessings and boons of all the fairies came true. She was kind, generous, clever and simply magical. Everyone loved her, the people of the kingdom, the birds and animals and even the plants!

And finally, it was the princess's sixteenth birthday. Her maid woke her up with a special bunch of flowers and a cheery song. The excited princess wore a pretty new gown and walked out into the warm sunshine to greet the happy day, sing along the chirping birds and play with her animal friends.

She walked quite a distance and came to a strange tower. She had never seen the broken down place before and wondered what it would be like inside it.

So the princess went up the long, winding staircase and came to a narrow room. As she stood in the doorway and looked inside, she saw an old hag busily spinning with a spindle. "What are you doing, dear lady?" she asked, for she had never before seen a spindle.

"It's called spinning, my child," said the old woman, with an ugly toothless smile. "Come, I'll show you how it's done."

The princess went ahead eagerly and hardly had she begun, that she pricked her finger on the needle and fell to the ground.

The wicked laughter of the thirteenth fairy echoed through the entire kingdom. Yes, it was she who had disguised herself as an old woman and tricked the princess.

The curse had come true.

But the twelfth good fairy's boon to the princess also had to work. So the princess did not die, but only fell into a deep sleep which would last a hundred years. The good fairy went all around the kingdom and put everyone to sleep – the king and queen, the courtiers, the subjects, the animals and birds and even the plants – so that they would not miss their beloved princess.

Days, months and years passed. While the entire kingdom slept, a thorny hedge of briar roses grew around the castle, hiding it completely.

The legend of the cursed princess - who was now called Sleeping Beauty - and her sleeping kingdom, spread far and wide. Many a princes came, trying their luck, cutting through the thick hedge of roses but to no avail.

The hundred years came to an end, and as luck would have it, a truly handsome and brave prince heard about Sleeping Beauty. Magically, the briar rose bushes parted to make way for the handsome gallant on his horse.

He passed the sleeping kingdom, and the king and queen asleep on their throne, looking for the princess.

Finally, he came to the beautiful bower where the fairies had laid her to sleep. So struck was the prince by her beauty, that he couldn't help but kiss Sleeping Beauty gently.

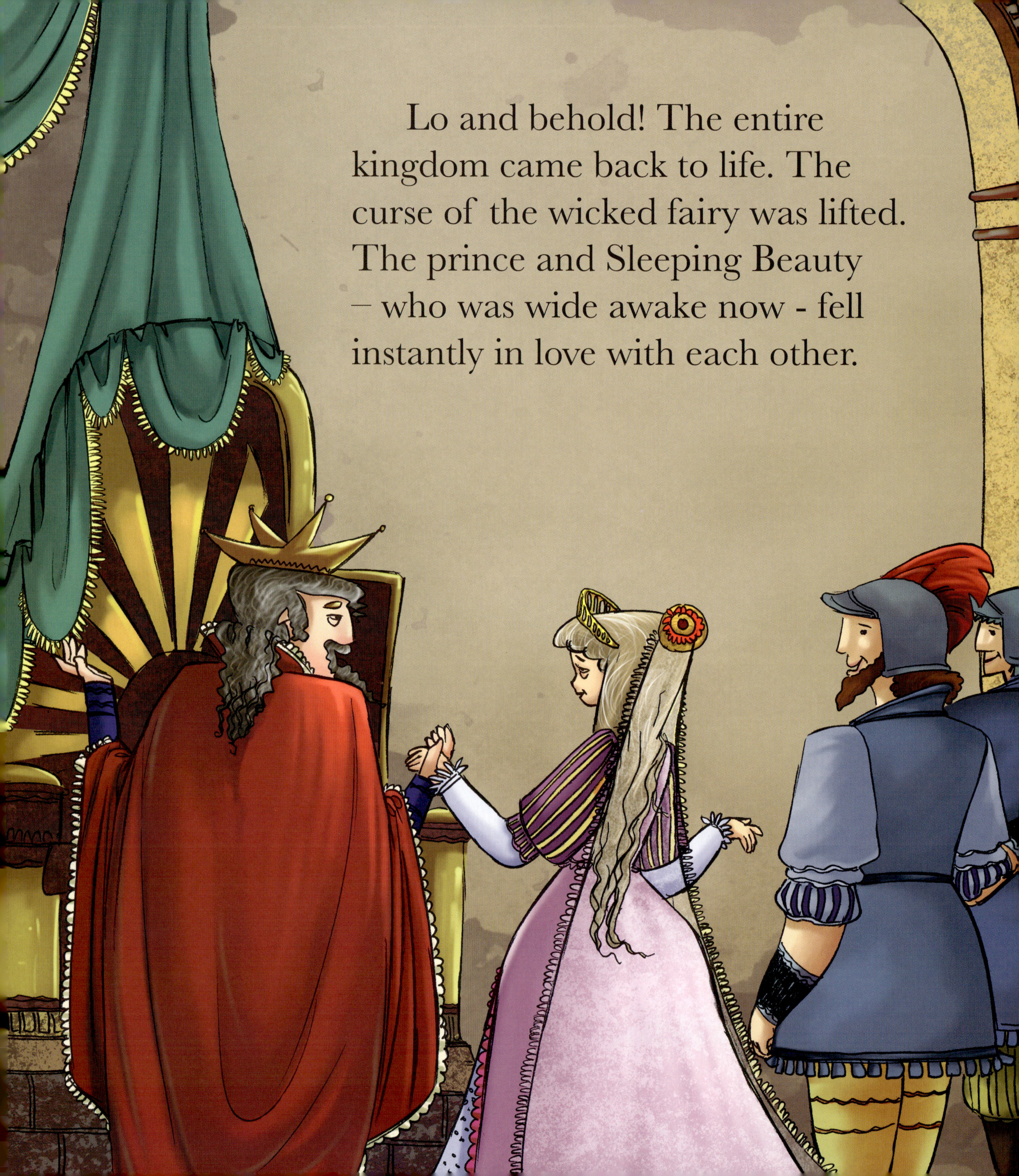

Lo and behold! The entire kingdom came back to life. The curse of the wicked fairy was lifted. The prince and Sleeping Beauty – who was wide awake now - fell instantly in love with each other.

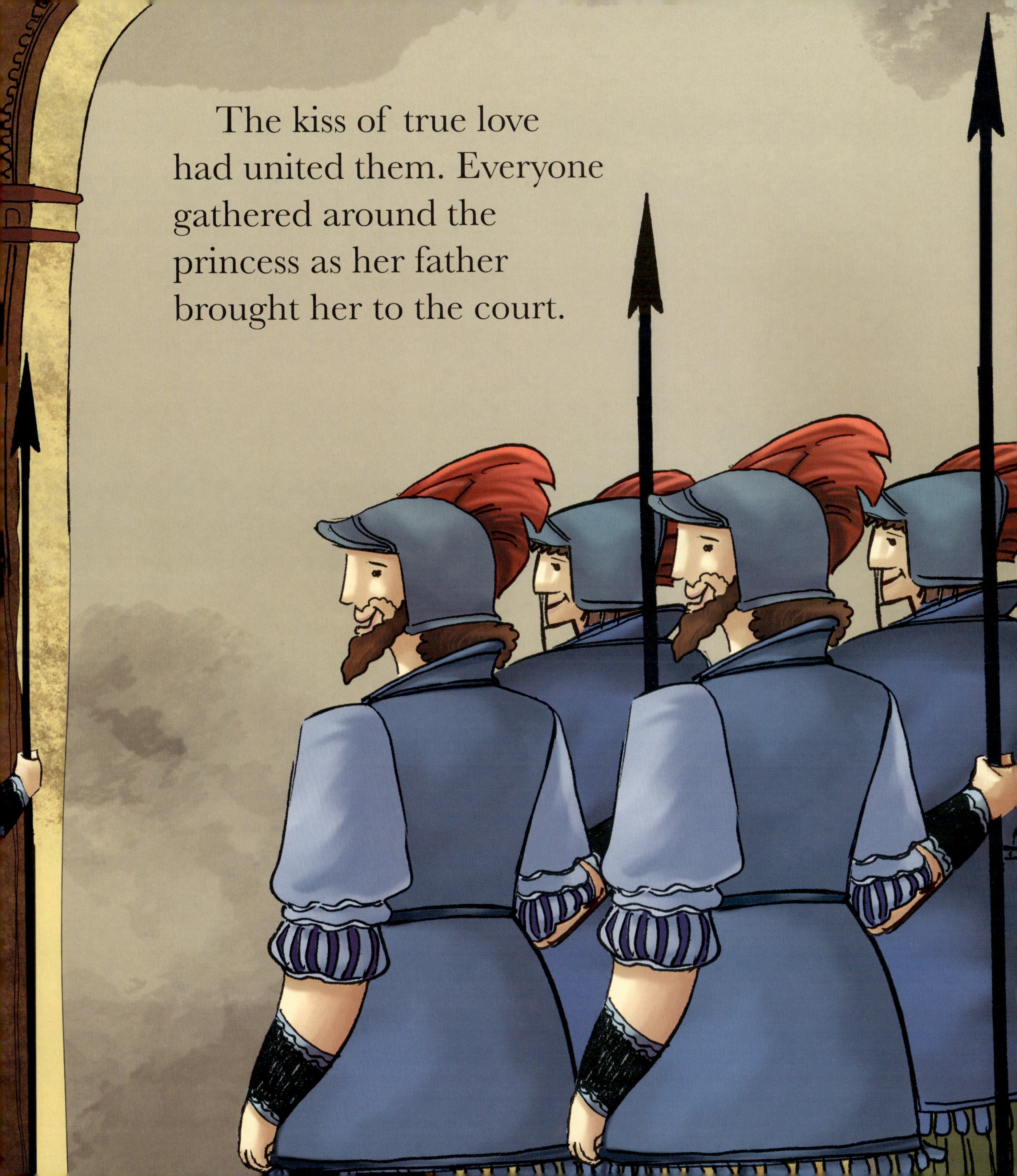

The kiss of true love had united them. Everyone gathered around the princess as her father brought her to the court.

And then, as all fairy tales end, the charming prince and the beautiful princess were married and lived happily ever after!